The Singing Shell

and The Naughty Smoke Fairies

illustrated by

Martine Blaney

AWARD PUBLICATIONS LIMITED

The Singing Shell

Once upon a time there was a brownie who lived underneath a mountain, far inland. He had never been further than his mountain.

He had been to the bottom and seen the river that wound its way along the green valley.

He had been to the top and shivered in the snow that always capped the tall mountain.

Every time he had climbed to the top there had been clouds there – great white mists that swirled around him so that he could see no further than a few metres before him. But one fine summer's day there were no clouds at all.

The brownie climbed to the top, panting and puffing, for the way was long and steep. He was surprised to see no white mists, but he did not look round until he reached the very top.

And then what a sight he saw! At his feet the whole countryside lay smiling in

the sun! Green meadows, yellow fields of corn, dark woods, blue hills in the distance, silver rivers winding slowly along.

And beyond, far beyond, lay something else, something that shone and glittered.

'What's that?' said the brownie to the eagle who lived on the mountain-top.

The eagle gazed at the shining thing and said:

'That is the sea, the great, wide, singing sea. You should visit it, brownie, and make friends with the mermaids and mermen. They are your cousins.'

So the brownie packed his bag and went down the mountain.

He followed green valley after green valley and at last he came to the sea.

There were hundreds of children there, paddling, bathing and digging. The brownie hid behind a rock and watched them. Then he slipped into a pool and went to seek his sea cousins.

He spent the whole summer by the sea, playing with the mermaids and mermen. He made himself a slippery suit of seaweed and a necklace of shells. Once he even played with some children, and they didn't guess he was a brownie. He had a perfectly lovely time, and grew as brown as his name!

But the longest of holidays must come to an end.

The day came when the brownie had to say goodbye to his new friends and go back to his mountain-home. He was sad, and he wept tears into a pool.

'I wish I could take the sea with me!' he said. 'I wish I could take the lovely, lovely sound of the endless waves breaking and sighing on the sands! If only I could!'

'We'll give you the sound of the sea for a parting present,' said a mermaid, and she picked up a big, curly shell. She let a little wave break into it, and then she emptied out the salt water and gave the shell to the brownie. 'Put it to your ear,' she said. 'Whenever you long for the sea, listen to your shell. You will hear it there!'

And sure enough, when the brownie held the big shell to his ear, he heard the sighing of the waves inside! How delighted he was! 'Sh-sh!' sang the shell. 'Sh-sh, sh-sh-sh!'

He took it home with him and put it on his mantelpiece in his cave beneath the mountain.

Every time he longed for the sea he put the shell to his ear and heard the lovely sound of the waves.

And the strange thing is that ever since that day all big shells have the sound of the sea inside them – a lovely, magical sound that anyone can hear.

The Naughty Smoke Fairies

Once upon a time a crowd of tiny little smoke fairies escaped from a bonfire. No one saw them go, and they took good care not to be seen as they slipped away into the open fields.

'Hurray!' said one, turning head over heels. 'Now we're free of that nasty old fire!'

'Yes, and we've got no work to do,' shouted another, swinging on a big daisy, and leaving little black marks on its white petals.

They were dreadfully black little fairies, as black as soot, for, of course, they had lived in smoke all their lives, because their duty was to take the horrid black smoke away from where children breathe, right up into the air among the clouds.

'Let's have some fun, and be really naughty,' said a third little fairy. 'I'm so tired of always being good and doing my work properly.'

'Yes, let's!' said all the others.

Presently the smoke fairies came to a large ring where toadstools grew. There they found fairy carpenters busy at work putting the toadstools in a ring so that the fairies might dance inside, and sit on the toadstools for supper.

'Oh, just look,' whispered one of the smoke fairies, pointing to an oak tree.

The others looked. The oak tree had, at the bottom by the roots, a little door leading into a cupboard. In this cupboard were stored all the lovely things for the party, cakes and sweets, jellies and honey-dew drinks.

'Do you think we might come to the party?' the smoke fairies asked the carpenters.

'Not if you haven't been invited,' answered the busy workers.

'We haven't been asked,' said a smoke fairy sadly.

'You are very naughty to be here then,' said the carpenter severely. 'If you haven't got a holiday for the party, then you should be at work.'

'Oh, bother!' cried the smoke fairies crossly. 'We *shan't* go back to work and we'll be as naughty as we can, so there!'

'Well, goodbye,' said the carpenters, flying off. 'We're going to get ready for the party.'

The smoke fairies sat down and frowned. 'Let's do something very, *very* bad,' said one. 'It's not fair that we haven't been asked.'

'I know!' exclaimed a tiny little black fairy. 'Let's saw the toadstools halfway through, so that when the fairies sit on them tonight, they'll all break, and tumble them off!'

'Oh yes, what fun!' said the naughty little fairies. They picked up some of the saws that the carpenters had left, and soon had all the toadstools sawn halfway through.

'I'm so hungry,' sighed the biggest fairy.

'Let's have a jelly out of the oak tree cupboard!' suggested another.

They all peeped into the cupboard, and chose something to eat. And what do you think – they were so dreadfully hungry that, in about ten minutes, they had eaten *every single thing* in that cupboard!

Then they all flew up into the trees, to watch the fairy dance.

One by one all the fairy guests arrived, and presently the King and Queen arrived too. Then the dancing began, and merrily the little fairies stepped into the fairy ring.

When the signal was given for supper, the smoke fairies began to feel uncomfortable, for 'Oh dear!' cried a little fairy, tumbling off a broken toadstool!

'Oh dear!' cried another.
'Oh dear!' cried a third.
One by one all the toadstools broke, and the astonished little fairies found themselves on the grass.

The King stood up, looking angry to think that such a trick had been played on the fairies.

Just then some little red fairies cried out, 'Your Majesty! the cupboard is empty, and there is nothing to eat!'

'Who has done these naughty things?' thundered the King.

There was no answer, but the smoke fairies began to feel very afraid up in the tree.

'If you please,' said a blue and white fairy, 'I believe it's some smoke fairies who have escaped from their work.'

'Oh, there they are, there they are!' shouted a yellow fairy, pointing up into the oak tree.

The smoke fairies, now thoroughly frightened, flew off as fast as they could, with all the others after them. They came to a field where there were a lot of red poppies. Very quickly each smoke fairy crept inside a poppy and closed the red petals round, and waited there, hidden.

But alas! the King and Queen soon found them, and made them come out.

'Now, tell me why you have been so naughty,' said the King.

'Please, Your Majesty,' said the biggest smoke fairy, 'it's because we were tired of our work, and we wanted to come to the party, and couldn't.'

'That is your own fault,' said the King.

'I sent you all an invitation, but my messenger found you had run away from your work, and so he couldn't give it to you.'

The smoke fairies began to cry.

'Oh, we *are* so sorry we've spoilt your party too! Please forgive us, and we'll go back to our work!'

'I'll forgive you,' answered the King kindly; 'and I will give you some other work to do if you are tired of carrying the smoke up into the air. You shall polish the black beetles for me every morning, and sleep in the poppies at night.'

'Oh, thank you, thank you,' cried the little smoke fairies, jumping back into their poppies.

'Goodbye,' said the King, and back they all went to finish the dance.

So those little smoke fairies live in the poppies now, and if you look into the middle of one, perhaps you can guess why it is so *very* black, and why, when you touch it, black, sooty powder comes off on your fingers!

ISBN 0-86163-708-9

The Singing Shell first published in *Book of the Year*
The Naughty Smoke Fairies first published in
Pinkity's Pranks and Other Nature Fairy Tales

This edition first published 1995 by Award Publications Limited,
27 Longford Street, London NW1 3DZ

Printed in Italy